Dear Parents:

Congratulations! Your child is taking the first steps on an exciting journey. The destination? Independent reading!

STEP INTO READING® will help your child get there. The program offers five steps to reading success. Each step includes fun stories and colorful art or photographs. In addition to original fiction and books with favorite characters, there are Step into Reading Non-Fiction Readers, Phonics Readers and Boxed Sets, Sticker Readers, and Comic Readers—a complete literacy program with something to interest every child.

Learning to Read, Step by Step!

Ready to Read   Preschool–Kindergarten
• big type and easy words • rhyme and rhythm • picture clues
For children who know the alphabet and are eager to begin reading.

Reading with Help   Preschool–Grade 1
• basic vocabulary • short sentences • simple stories
For children who recognize familiar words and sound out new words with help.

Reading on Your Own   Grades 1–3
• engaging characters • easy-to-follow plots • popular topics
For children who are ready to read on their own.

Reading Paragraphs   Grades 2–3
• challenging vocabulary • short paragraphs • exciting stories
For newly independent readers who read simple sentences with confidence.

Ready for Chapters   Grades 2–4
• chapters • longer paragraphs • full-color art
For children who want to take the plunge into chapter books but still like colorful pictures.

STEP INTO READING® is designed to give every child a successful reading experience. The grade levels are only guides; children will progress through the steps at their own speed, developing confidence in their reading.

Remember, a lifetime love of reading starts with a single step!

Visit us on the Web!
StepIntoReading.com
rhcbooks.com

Educators and librarians, for a variety of teaching tools, visit us at RHTeachersLibrarians.com

ISBN 978-0-593-12372-0 (trade) — ISBN 978-0-593-12373-7 (lib. bdg.)

Printed in the United States of America   10 9 8 7 6 5 4 3 2 1

adapted by Christy Webster

based on the teleplay "Pizza Pit" by Brian Posehn

illustrated by Patrick Spaziante

Random House 🏠 New York

The moon was full.

It looked like a pizza.

That could only mean one thing.

It was pizza week!

The Turtles would eat pizza

at their four favorite pizza places.

First, they went to Mikey's favorite,

Lou Mike-Tony's.

But when they got there, they saw . . .

. . . it had fallen into a sinkhole!

"I think it is closed," Leo said.

Mikey was devastated.

Next, they went to Donnie's favorite,
Tony Lou's.
But just when they arrived . . .

. . . Tony Lou's sank, too!

Now the Turtles were suspicious.

Was someone taking out pizza places?

Their favorite pizza places?

The Turtles were suspicious *and* hungry.

They needed to get to the next
pizza place—
and fast.
To the Shell Hogs!

Leo's favorite pizza place,

Mike Tony's,

was still there.

"Everything is fine," Raph said.

Everything was not fine.

Customers ran out screaming.

Three mean mutants

chased them out.

Riding their Shell Hogs,
the Turtles chased the mutants
down a tunnel.
The Groundhog dug fast.

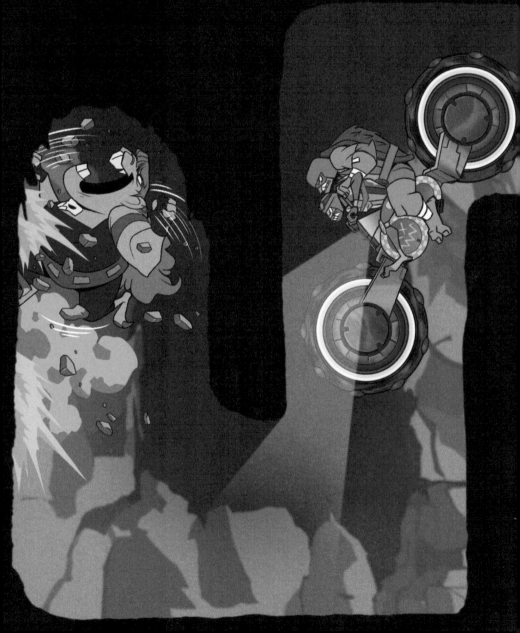

The Honey Badger
tricked Donnie and Leo.

Finally, they busted into a big cavern.

It was under the pizza place.

The Prairie Dog put

huge amps on a big pillar.

She plugged in her guitar.

She sent a sound wave

through the pillar.

Then she ran away.

The sound wave sank

Mike Tony's.

Raph would not give up.

"Pizza week is about

coming together

and eating pizza," he said.

Then Raph realized

that his favorite

pizza place was next!

The Turtles raced
to Mike Lou's.
They got the customers
to leave before
the mean mutants arrived.

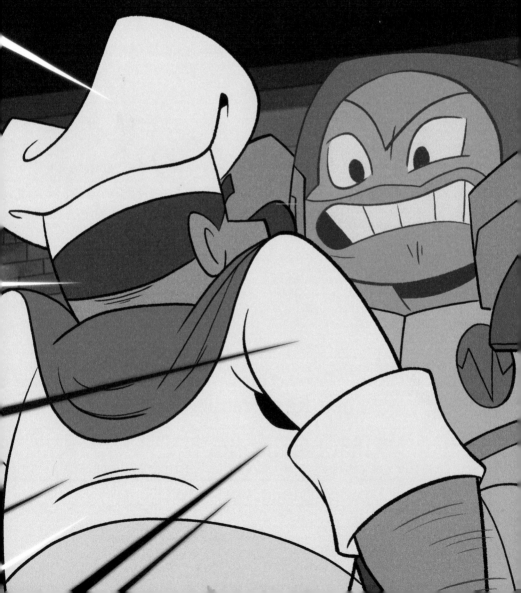

Under Mike Lou's,
the Turtles found the mutants.
They attacked!

"Why are you ruining pizza week?" Donnie shouted.

"Who cares about pizza?" Prairie Dog said.

They were trying to destroy the pillars under the city.

They were a band called Digg.
They wanted to sink
a stadium and play underground
for thousands of people.

"You just want to play a gig?"

Raph asked.

"We do not even like pizza,"

Prairie Dog said.

Mikey was furious.

But Raph had an idea.

The owners of the four pizza places came together.
They opened a new pizza place.
It was better than ever!

On opening night,
they had special guests
play a show.

Raph had been right.

Pizza week brought people together.